Mr. APPLE'S Family

by

Jean McDevitt

Illustrated by NINON
Cover illustration by NINON and Nada Serafimovic
Cover design by Tina DeKam
First published in 1950
This unabridged version has updated grammar and spelling.

This book is
affectionately dedicated to
THE PRIMARY CHILDREN OF
THE KIMBERLY SCHOOL

Table of Contents

Chapter 1

Mr. Apple Names the Children

Mr. and Mrs. Apple lived in the city. They lived in a little apartment in a big apartment house. They had lived there a long time. When Mr. and Mrs. Apple first went to live in the city, there were not any little Apples. Now there were five little Apples.

The oldest Apple boy was named MacIntosh. This was Mr. Apple's idea. He said there was no use having a name like Apple if you just called your children by ordinary names. "George Apple or Tom Apple or Jack Apple would not do at all," said Mr. Apple. So the Apple children were named for real apples.

Mrs. Apple did not like this idea of Mr. Apple's very much.

"MacIntosh is much too big a name for a tiny baby," said Mrs. Apple.

"He will not be a tiny baby long," said Mr. Apple. "We will call him Mac for short."

Mrs. Apple saw that Mr. Apple wanted very much to call the baby MacIntosh. "Very well," said Mrs. Apple. "We will call him Mac." She knew she could not have her own way all the time. Mr. Apple must sometimes have what he wanted. So when the second little Apple came, he was named Jonathan. He was called Jon for short.

Mrs. Apple got used to the idea of MacIntosh and Jonathan for her two boys. She even boasted a little bit to the neighbors.

"Mr. Apple is very clever," Mrs. Apple would say. "He has such fine ideas. No one but a man as clever as Mr. Apple would have thought of naming his children for real apples."

Then the first little girl came along. It was much harder for Mr. Apple to think of an apple name for a little girl.

"If she had been a boy," said Mr. Apple, "I could have named her Spitzenberg. She could have been Spitz for short."

"She is not a boy, and she cannot be named Spitzenberg," said Mrs. Apple. "A little girl should have a pretty name. She cannot be called Spitz."

"How would Delicious be?" asked Mr. Apple. "There is a fine apple named Delicious."

"Delicious is a beautiful name," said Mrs. Apple happily. "I think we will call her Delia for short."

The fourth little Apple was also a girl. Mr. Apple had a very hard time indeed to find an apple name for her. He thought and thought about it. But he could not think of an apple name for another little girl.

One day Mr. Apple said to Mrs. Apple, "I know what I will do. I will go to the library and look for a name in a book."

"In a book!" said Mrs. Apple. "Is there a book with apple names in it?"

"Yes," said Mr. Apple. "I am sure there is. There is a book for everything in the library."

So Mr. Apple went to the public library. He said to the librarian, "Have you a book that will tell me the names of apples?"

8

"Yes, indeed," said the librarian. "We have a Garden Encyclopedia."

Mr. Apple took the big book and sat down at a table. He hunted and hunted through it for an apple name for his second little girl. He wrote many names on a piece of paper. Then he took the Garden Encyclopedia back to the librarian.

"Thank you for your help," said Mr. Apple.

"Did you find what you wanted?" asked the librarian.

"Well," said Mr. Apple, "I found a great many names, but they are not very good names for a little girl."

The librarian looked very surprised. "I thought you wanted names of apples," she said.

"So I did, so I did," answered Mr. Apple.

He did not stop to explain. He wanted to get home. He wanted to see if Mrs. Apple would like any of the names he had found.

"Did you find a book of apple names?" asked Mrs. Apple as soon as Mr. Apple came home.

"Oh yes," said Mr. Apple. "There is a big, big book of apple names in the library. It is called a Garden Encyclopedia."

"It was very clever of you to think of going to the library, Mr. Apple," said Mrs. Apple.

"That is what a library is for," said Mr. Apple.

"What names did you find?" asked Mrs. Apple anxiously.

"Well," said Mr. Apple, "that is the trouble. There were many fine apple names for little boys. If she were a boy, we could call her Fall Pippin or Baldwin. I am very fond of Baldwin apples," said Mr. Apple. "If she were only a boy, I would name her Baldwin. We could call her Baldy for short."

"She is not a boy," said Mrs. Apple. "And she cannot be called Baldwin. She cannot be called Baldy. She is a sweet little girl. I am glad she is a girl. I like little girls."

"I like little girls, too," said Mr. Apple. "But it is so hard to find good names for them."

Mrs. Apple did not say that, of course, the baby could be called Nancy or Mary or Elizabeth. She did not want to hurt Mr. Apple's feelings.

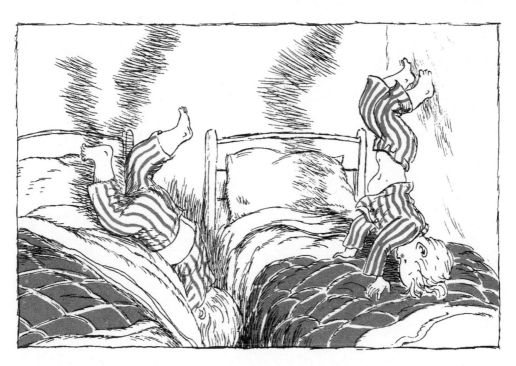

"What were some of the other names in the Garden Encyclopedia?" asked Mrs. Apple.

"There is an apple called a Snow Apple," said Mr. Apple.

"Snow Apple," said Mrs. Apple. "Snow Apple," she said again. "That is very pretty. I think we will name the baby Snow. She will not need a nickname."

Mr. Apple was very pleased that Mrs. Apple liked one of the names he had found. Snow was a good name for the baby. She had very white skin and bright red cheeks. She looked very much like a little round snow apple. Mr. and Mrs. Apple were very happy to have found just the right name for the fourth little Apple.

After a while the fifth little Apple came. The fifth little Apple was a girl, too! Poor Mr. Apple was quite upset again.

"Oh dear, oh dear," he said. "I cannot possibly think of another apple name for a little girl."

"Why not go to the library again?" asked Mrs. Apple.

"No, it would not do any good," said Mr. Apple. "I wrote down all the apple names there were in the Garden Encyclopedia. There was not another name for a little girl."

"Well," said Mrs. Apple, "four of our children have apple names. Why not just name this one Nancy or Mary or Elizabeth?"

"No, no," said Mr. Apple. "Those names will not do for an Apple child. I do wish I could think of an apple name for another little girl."

"There!" said Mrs. Apple in excitement. "An Apple—An Apple."

Mr. Apple looked at Mrs. Apple in great surprise.

"What do you mean by saying 'an apple' over and over again?" he asked.

"Why, don't you see?" replied Mrs. Apple. "We can call the fifth baby An Apple. We will spell it A-n-n. Ann Apple is her name."

Now, Mr. Apple saw that Mrs. Apple wanted very much to call the little girl Ann. He did not like this idea of Mrs. Apple's so very much. But Mr. Apple knew that he could not always have what he wanted. Mrs. Apple must sometimes

have what she wanted. So Mr. Apple said, "Ann Apple is not a bad name. At least it makes sense. Nancy Apple or Mary Apple or Elizabeth Apple would not make sense at all."

So the fifth and last little Apple had a real little girl's name, and that pleased Mrs. Apple very much indeed.

20

Chapter 2

Mrs. Apple Goes House Hunting

"Mr. Apple," said Mrs. Apple one night in spring, "the time has come when we must move. We cannot live in this little apartment any longer."

"Move!" said Mr. Apple in surprise. "Why must we move? We have lived here a long time."

"There is not room for so many little Apples here. There is not room for them to play. There is not room for all the toys," said Mrs. Apple.

Now, Mr. Apple knew that Mrs. Apple was right, because he was always bumping into one toy or another. That very night he had bumped into Mac's wagon in the hall. He had stumbled over Jon's trains in the living room. He had tripped over Delia's doll carriage in the dining room. He had knocked down Snow's block house in the kitchen, and he had stepped on Ann's rattle in the nursery!

"You are right, Mrs. Apple," said Mr. Apple, "but where can we move?"

"We can move to the country," answered Mrs. Apple. "I shall go house hunting tomorrow."

The next morning, Mrs. Apple put on her best blue hat with the red feather on it. She said goodbye to Mac and Jon, to Delia and Snow, and Baby Ann, who were all staying with a neighbor for the day. She took the train to the country.

Mrs. Apple had a busy day—a very busy day. She looked for houses all day long. She looked at brown houses and gray houses. She looked at white houses, and she looked at yellow houses, but she could not find a house that was just right. Some houses were too big, and some were too little.

Late in the afternoon, Mrs. Apple came to the end of the village. She turned down a country lane, and then Mrs. Apple stood still. She stood still for a whole minute, looking, looking, looking. Soon Mrs. Apple began to run. She ran to the end of the lane.

25

At the end of the lane was an orchard full of crooked little trees. The trees were all covered with little pink blossoms. They were apple trees. In the very middle of the orchard was a house. It was a funny little house with a funny crooked roof, funny crooked windows, and a funny crooked chimney. On the funny little house was a big sign. It said, "For Sale"

in funny crooked letters. Down in one corner, it said, "Key at Mr. Jake's Store."

Mrs. Apple peeked in one of the front windows. She peeked in one of the side windows, and she climbed up on a big rock to peek in one of the back windows. Then she went back down the lane just as fast as she could go to Mr. Jake's grocery store.

Mr. Jake's grocery store was a tiny white store at the other end of the lane.

28

"How very convenient it will be to have a store so near," said Mrs. Apple to herself.

"May I please have the key to the house in the apple orchard?" Mrs. Apple said to the man in the store.

"Yes, indeed you may," said Mr. Jake. "Do you want to buy a house?" he asked.

"Yes," said Mrs. Apple. "I am sure I want to buy this house, but I must see the inside first."

"It is a funny little house," said Mr. Jake, "but it is a good house. It has a good roof, and it has strong walls, but it has a great many apple trees around it. Do you like apples?"

"Of course, we like apples," said Mrs. Apple a little crossly. "We are an Apple family. I am Mrs. Apple, and there are Mr. Apple and five little Apples at home in the city."

"Then it is just the house for you," said Mr. Jake.

"I think so, too," said Mrs. Apple.

She took the key and went back to the funny, crooked little house. She unlocked the front door and went in. She went from room to room. She went down funny crooked little

stairs to the cellar. She went up funny crooked little stairs to the attic.

"What a fine place for the children to play on rainy days," said Mrs. Apple when she saw the attic. "This is just the house for us. I do hope Mr. Apple will like it."

Then Mrs. Apple took the key back to Mr. Jake. "Thank you for the key," she said. "I must catch a train back to the city now. I will bring Mr. Apple to see the house on Sunday."

"I will take you to the train in my wagon," said Mr. Jake. "I am going to take a load of vegetables to the station."

"Thank you very much," said Mrs. Apple.

Mr. Jake's wagon was all loaded with bunches of red radishes, bunches and bunches of little green onions, and bunches and bunches and bunches of green asparagus. Mrs. Apple climbed up onto the seat beside Mr. Jake. Mr. Jake said, "Giddy up," to his two big white horses, and they went down the road to the station.

34

Chapter 3

The New Home

That night when Mrs. Apple got home from the country, she told Mr. Apple all about the house in the apple orchard.

"It is just the house for an Apple family to live in," said Mrs. Apple. "It has apple trees all around it. There is a big room in the attic where the children can play. They can keep all their toys there. You will not bump into their wagons and blocks. You will not stumble over the doll carriage or step on Baby Ann's rattle."

"It sounds like a fine home for us," said Mr. Apple. "I should love to live in an apple orchard, but how much does it cost?"

Now, Mrs. Apple had been so excited and so pleased to find the house in the apple orchard that she had forgotten to ask Mr. Jake how much it would cost. Mrs. Apple did not think very much about money.

"We are rich because we have so many children; we do not need so much money," she would say.

Mr. Apple did not agree with Mrs. Apple about this at all. When Mrs. Apple took all five little Apples to buy new shoes or new coats, Mr. Apple thought that it would be very nice indeed to have more money. Still, he would

rather have his five little Apples than all the money in the world, and he could earn enough to pay for what they needed, so he did not complain.

"We will go to see the house on Sunday," said Mr. Apple. "We can find out how much it costs then."

So the very next Sunday, Mr. and Mrs. Apple drove their little old car to the country. When they turned into the lane, Mrs. Apple watched

Mr. Apple's face. She wanted very much to have Mr. Apple like the house in the apple orchard as much as she did.

Mr. Apple did like it. As soon as he saw the little house with the apple trees all around it, he smiled a broad smile.

"This is a very fine home that you have found for us, Mrs. Apple," said Mr. Apple. "I do hope that I can afford to buy it. I must go to see Mr. Jake right away. I must find out how much it costs."

"Look at the house first," said Mrs. Apple.

"No," said Mr. Apple. "I know I shall like the house if you like it. I must find out the price."

So Mr. Apple went to Mr. Jake's grocery store. Mr. Jake lived in a little white house next to the store. He came to the door.

"I am Mr. Apple," said Mr. Apple to Mr. Jake. "How much is the house in the apple orchard?"

"It is five thousand dollars," said Mr. Jake.

"Five thousand dollars!" said Mr. Apple. "That is a great deal of money."

"There are a great many apple trees around it," said Mr. Jake. "You can sell the apples to help pay for the house."

41

"Perhaps I could," said Mr. Apple thoughtfully, "but there may not be enough apples. I don't know much about growing apples. If I was sure the apples would grow well, I would buy the house. It is just the right home for my family."

"There are so many blossoms on the trees, there should be plenty of apples," answered Mr. Jake. "Why don't you rent the house for a year? Then, if you have a fine crop of apples, you could buy it."

"That is a wonderful idea. I will rent the house first. We will take good care of it, and I will learn all I can about growing apples."

Mrs. Apple was a little disappointed when Mr. Apple told her he could only rent the house. She would have liked to buy it at once, but she knew that Mr. Apple was right. She knew that they should not buy the house until they could pay for it.

44

"The house costs a great deal of money," explained Mr. Apple. "I cannot buy it until I see how many apples there are on the trees. If there are enough apples to sell, I will buy it next year."

"We will all help," said Mrs. Apple. "Mac and Jon can pick the apples, but we must not sell all the apples. Apples are so good for the children."

"I hope there will be enough apples to sell and enough apples to eat. I shall get some books from the library so I can read about how to grow fine apples," said Mr. Apple.

So that is how it happened that one sunny day, a big green moving van full of furniture left the apartment house in the city where the Apple family had lived.

The little old car was full of all the things the van could not hold. Three dolls, a big teddy bear, and a toy truck were on top of a basket of Mrs. Apple's best china. The basket was on the back seat beside Mrs. Apple and Baby Ann. Delia's doll carriage had to be tied onto the

back of the car. Mac's skis and Jon's sled were tied onto the roof of the car. Delia held a big toy giraffe on her lap in the front seat beside Snow and Mr. Apple. The giraffe's head stuck out of the window. The little old car was just as full as it could be.

"If this car was a sleigh, we would look like Santa Claus," said Delia.

"We certainly do look like Santa Claus," said Mr. Apple.

He did not really enjoy driving along the city streets with his car so full of toys. He did not really enjoy driving along the country roads looking like Santa Claus. But Mr. Apple knew he could not always have what he wanted. The children must sometimes have what they wanted. The children wanted their toys, so Mr. Apple drove his car loaded with toys after the big green moving van. He drove his car loaded with toys into the lane by the apple orchard and stopped it behind the van.

Soon all the furniture and toys had been carried into the little house in the apple orchard. Mr. and Mrs. Apple and all the little Apples were very tired after such a busy day, so they went to bed early. It was so quiet in the country that they went to sleep at once. Baby Ann did not wake up all night.

The wind blew the apple blossoms gently
against the house. The moon shone on the
apple trees and on the ground covered with
apple blossoms. The children slept on and on
with the fresh country air blowing on their
faces through the crooked little windows of
the funny, crooked little house in the apple
orchard.

Chapter 4

Painting the House

For a few days the Apples worked very hard getting their home settled. Mrs. Apple washed the white woodwork and scrubbed the floors until the little house was as shiny and clean as a house could be. She hung up pretty ruffled curtains at the crooked little windows and put some red geraniums on the window sills.

Delia and Snow washed all the dishes and put them away in the cupboard. Mac and Jon took the rugs outdoors and swept them and beat them until all the city dust was gone. Then they spread the rugs on the floor and straightened the furniture.

Baby Ann got out her blocks, and soon they were scattered over the clean rug, but Mrs. Apple did not mind that.

"It looks like home now," she said happily. "It looks like a real Apple house inside. I wish it looked like an Apple house outside, too. That green paint is so dingy."

"Could we paint it ourselves?" asked Mac.

"That would be fun," said Jon. "I want to help paint the outside of the house!"

"What a good idea," answered Mrs. Apple. "You could paint it red. An Apple family should live in a red house. I am sure Father

Apple will think so, too. I will speak to him about it tonight."

So one night soon after that, Mr. Apple came home from the city with his hands full. He was carrying a big can of red paint in one hand. He was carrying a big can of green paint in the other hand. He had a bundle of paintbrushes under his arm.

Mac and Jon ran to meet him. Delia and Snow ran to meet him, too.

"I have brought some paint so we can paint the outside of the house," said Mr. Apple.

Mac took the can of red paint. Jon took the can of green paint.

"Hurrah!" said Mac. "Red paint for the house."

"Hurrah!" said Jon. "Green paint for the roof."

"Hurrah!" said Delia and Snow. "Paint brushes to paint the house with."

"I want to paint the roof," said Mac.

"I want to paint the roof, too," said Jon.

"You may paint the roof," said Mr. Apple. He did not like the idea of climbing up on the roof himself. He thought Mac and Jon would be much better at that.

"Tomorrow is Saturday, and I do not have to go to the city," said Mr. Apple. "We will begin to paint the house tomorrow. Mac and Jon may paint the roof. Delia and Snow may paint the low places on the house. I will climb the ladder and paint the high places."

The next morning Mr. and Mrs. Apple and all the little Apples got up very early. They put

on their oldest clothes. Mac and Jon wanted to start painting at once.

"May we begin to paint now?" they asked as soon as they were dressed.

"No," said Mrs. Apple. "You must have your breakfast first."

So they all ate a good breakfast of hot cereal and milk, orange juice, and toast. Then they were ready to work.

Mr. Apple put the ladder up against the house. Mac and Jon got some sticks of wood to stir the paint. Mac stirred the red paint. Jon stirred the green paint. They stirred and stirred the paint until it was all smooth.

"Now we are ready to paint the house," said Mr. Apple.

Mac took the can of green paint. He was up the ladder and onto the very top of the roof in no time. Jon took two big paint brushes. He climbed up the ladder after Mac as fast as he could.

The boys began to paint the roof. They painted very fast. Soon spatters of green paint began flying around. Spatters of green paint came down on Mr. Apple, who was standing on the ladder. Spatters of green paint came down on Delia and Snow, who were painting the low places on the house. Spatters of green paint even came down on Baby Ann, who was sitting under an apple tree, and on Mrs. Apple, who was watching Mr. Apple and the children paint the house.

"Boys, boys," called Mr. Apple. "That is not the way to paint. You must paint slowly. You must paint carefully. Watch me. I will teach you how to paint."

Mr. Apple put his brush in the red paint. He dipped his brush in the can halfway. Then he

turned it up quickly and began to paint slowly
back and forth, back and forth.

"I see," said Mac.

"I see, too," said Jon.

The boys began to paint again. They painted
carefully this time. Delia and Snow painted
carefully, too.

Back and forth went Mac's and Jon's brushes on the roof. Back and forth went Mr. Apple's brush on the high places of the house. Back and forth went Delia's and Snow's brushes on the low places of the house. It did not take very many Saturdays to finish painting the little old house, with so many careful helpers.

When the house was all painted, Mr. and Mrs. Apple and the five little Apples were very proud of it. The house looked so bright and shiny with its fresh red paint and green roof.

"Now it is a real Apple house," said Mrs. Apple happily. "It is all clean and white inside, and it is all red and shiny outside."

By the time the Apples had finished painting the house, the apple blossoms had gone from the trees. Little green apples had begun to grow on the branches where the apple blossoms had been. The Apple family hoped more than ever that they could soon buy the little house and have it for their very own always.

68

Chapter 5

Mac and Jon Find Some Pets

One day Mac and Jon were cutting the grass around the house. The grass was very long. Mac had the lawn mower, and Jon had a rake. Back and forth went Mac with his lawn mower. Back and forth went Jon with his rake. It was very hard work.

"I know what we need," said Mac.

"What?" asked Jon.

"We need some animals to help us cut the

grass," said Mac.

"How could animals push a lawn mower?" asked Snow, who was watching them work.

"They could not push a lawn mower," answered Mac, "but they could eat the grass. I wish we had a lamb to help us keep the grass short."

"A goat would help, too," said Jon. "I wish I had a goat. We could build a little wagon for him. When he was not eating grass, we could drive him. We could drive him to school in the fall, and we could drive him to Mr. Jake's store to get the groceries."

"I am going to ask Father Apple for a goat," said Jon.

"I am going to ask him for a lamb," said Mac. That night when Mr. Apple came home,

71

Mac and Jon ran down the lane to meet him.

"May I have a lamb, Father?" asked Mac.

"May I have a goat, Father?" asked Jon.

"Dear me," said Mr. Apple in surprise. "Why do you want a lamb, MacIntosh? Why do you want a goat, Jonathan?" he asked. Mr. Apple liked to call the children by their full apple names sometimes.

"We want a goat and a lamb to help us keep the grass short," said Mac and Jon together.

"The grass is so long. It is so hard to cut," said Mac.

"Well, well," said Mr. Apple. "That is a splendid idea. Why didn't I think of that before? Now that we live in the country, of course, we should have some animals. I will ask Mr. Jake where we can get a lamb and a goat. You would still have to cut the grass around the house to keep it looking neat, but the animals could eat the grass and the clover in the apple orchard."

"Hurrah!" said Mac.

"Hurrah! Hurrah!" said Jon.

"May we go to ask Mr. Jake now?" asked Mac.

"Please, let us go right now," said Jon.

Now Mr. Apple had been working hard all day. He had been working hard to earn money to pay for the new home. He had been working hard to earn money to buy food for all the little

75

Apples. He did not really want to go down the lane to Mr. Jake's store right away. He wanted to rest, and he wanted to spray the apple trees before dinner.

"We can go after dinner just as well," said Mr. Apple. "We will go to see Mr. Jake right after dinner. I must spray the trees before dinner."

Mac looked at Jon. Jon looked at Mac. They wanted very much to go to see Mr. Jake right away about the lamb and the goat. They did not want to wait until after dinner. But the boys knew they could not always have what they wanted. Grownups must sometimes have what they wanted.

"All right," said Mac. "We will wait and go after dinner."

"Yes," said Jon. "We will go right after dinner."

So after dinner they all started off for Mr. Jake's store. Mac and Jon went so fast that Mr. Apple had to take great big steps to keep up with them. They found Mr. Jake sitting on a chair in front of the little white store, smoking his pipe.

"Good evening, Mr. Apple," said Mr. Jake. "Good evening, boys. Can I do something for you?"

"We hope you can," said Mr. Apple.

"I want to buy a lamb," said Mac.

"I want to buy a goat," said Jon.

"Can you tell us where we can find a goat and a lamb?" asked both boys together.

"Dear me," said Mr. Jake. "Why do you want a goat and a lamb?"

"To help us keep the grass short in the

orchard. A goat and a lamb would eat the grass so it would not grow so tall. We could build a little wagon for the goat. We could drive him to school."

"Goats and lambs like grass," said Mr. Jake. "That is a very clever idea. I was over at Farmer

Gray's house yesterday. He has goats, and he has lambs. Perhaps he would sell you one. I will walk over there with you."

"Hurrah!" said Mac.

"Hurrah!" said Jon.

Mr. Apple, Mr. Jake, and the boys set off across the fields to Farmer Gray's house. The boys ran ahead, and when Mr. Apple and Mr. Jake got there, Mac and Jon were talking fast to Farmer Gray, telling him why they wanted a goat and a lamb so very much.

"Well," said Farmer Gray, "you boys need a goat and a lamb to work for you. I need some boys to work for me. If you will come every day this summer and hunt eggs for me, and if you will deliver the eggs to my customers, I will give you a lamb and a goat."

"We will, we will!" shouted Mac and Jon.

"That is a bargain, then," said Farmer Gray. "Come with me and choose your own goat and your own lamb."

84

Mr. Apple and the boys followed Farmer Gray to a big field where six young goats were racing and chasing around. There was a low stone wall around the field. One little black-and-tan goat was walking on top of the wall. She lifted her feet daintily as she walked. Then, suddenly, as the boys came near, she began to run on the wall. She lifted her feet high in the air and ran in leaps and bounds. The little goat was very sure-footed. She always landed right on the wall after each leap and bound.

"Oh," said Jon, "that is a fine goat. May I have that one, Farmer Gray? I love that one."

"If you think you can manage her, you may have her," said the farmer. "She is a very lively goat, as you can see."

"I think I can manage her," said Jon.

"If you give her plenty of grass to eat, she will be happy," said Farmer Gray. "There is nonesuch a goat for eating grass."

"There will be plenty of grass in our orchard," Jon answered.

"Nonesuch, nonesuch," Mr. Apple muttered to himself.

Just then the goat jumped down from the wall and came running toward them. Farmer Gray picked a bunch of long grass and gave it to Jon. "Hold it out for the goat to eat while I fasten this rope around her so that you can lead her home."

The goat came right up to Jon and snapped at the grass, chewing away happily while the farmer took a rope from his pocket and fastened it around the goat's neck.

"Now we must find that lamb," said he, smiling at Mac.

Farmer Gray led the way to another field where some lambs were frolicking among the red clover. They were running and leaping and chasing one another around the field. That is, all of them were running and leaping and chasing except one little lamb. He was a round, chubby little lamb. He was so round and so chubby that he looked like a big white ball among the clover. He had a black nose and two black feet. He had one black spot under his chin. The lamb was eating the clover just

as fast as he could eat. Nibble, nibble, nibble, he went at the clover.

Mac stood watching the lambs a long time. He looked at each one carefully.

"Which one shall it be?" asked Farmer Gray at last.

"I should like to have the little fat one that is nibbling the clover," said Mac. "He looks like a good eater, and that is the kind of a lamb we

need. I like his curly coat and his black nose and his two black feet."

"He is yours, then," said the farmer. He went quietly up to the lamb and put a rope around his neck. The lamb kept right on nibbling the clover. But when the farmer tried to lead him to Mac, the lamb pulled back and tried to run away. Farmer Gray had to pick him up in his arms and carry him to Mac.

"Baa, b-a-a," said the lamb.

"He does not want to leave the clover field," said Farmer Gray. "I think he will walk along all

right when we get him away from the clover."

"I am going to name him Clover," said Mac.

"That would be a splendid name for that lamb," answered Farmer Gray.

"What shall I name my goat?" asked Jon.

"I know," said Mr. Apple. "Farmer Gray said there was nonesuch a goat for eating grass. I have been trying to think of what the word nonesuch reminded me. Now I remember. When one of your sisters came, I went to the library to look up a good apple name for her. There was an apple called 'Nonesuch.' That would be a fine name for your goat."

"Yes, it would," answered Jon. "I will call her Nonesuch."

Mr. Apple was very pleased to have thought of an apple name for the goat.

"I wish I could think of a good apple name for the lamb," said Mr. Apple. "How would 'Northern Spy' be? He is so clever at spying clover to eat."

"No," said Mac. "My lamb is not going to have an apple name. He is going to be called Clover."

"Well," said Mr. Apple, "he is your lamb, and you can call him anything you like." But Mr. Apple was a little disappointed just the same.

He loved apple names, although he knew he could not always have his own way about names. Mrs. Apple had decided on Baby Ann's name, and now Mac was choosing the name he wanted for his own lamb.

96

Chapter 6

The Apples Are Ripe

At first Nonesuch the goat was a great help to the Apple family. She ate and ate the grass in the orchard so that Mac and Jon did not have to cut it. Clover, the lamb, nibbled and nibbled the grass and nibbled and nibbled the clover under the apple trees.

Sometimes Nonesuch did not eat grass. She ate other things. One day she ate Baby Ann's shoe which had come off as she played in the apple orchard. One day she ate a big hole in Delia's red dress which Mrs. Apple had washed and hung on the line to dry.

"This will never do," said Mr. Apple. "Nonesuch must not eat the children's shoes. Shoes cost too much money. I cannot buy shoes for a goat to eat."

"Nonesuch must not eat the children's clothes," said Mrs. Apple to Jon. "You will have to watch your goat more carefully."

"I will," said Jon. "I will watch her more carefully."

Jon did watch the goat carefully after that, but he could not watch her all the time. He had to go to gather eggs for Farmer Gray every day to pay for the goat.

One day when Jon had gone with Mac to

gather eggs, Nonesuch grew tired of eating the grass in the orchard. The little green apples on the trees had grown and begun to turn red now. Some of the branches were quite low. Nonesuch saw the red apples. She reached her head up and began to eat the apples. She ate the apples until there were no more red apples on the lowest branches of the trees. She was just reaching her head up higher to eat the apples farther up when Mr. Apple turned in at the gate.

When Mr. Apple saw Nonesuch eating his fine red apples, he began to run. Nonesuch saw Mr. Apple coming. She was just taking a bite out of a big red apple. Nonesuch cocked her head on one side and looked at Mr. Apple. Then, with the apple still in her mouth, Nonesuch began to run, too. She ran around and around the apple trees, and Mr. Apple ran after her, but Mr. Apple could not run as fast as the goat could run. Poor Mr. Apple was all out of breath. Just then he saw Mac and Jon coming back from Farmer Gray's house.

"R-u-n, r-u-n," called Mr. Apple to the boys. "C-a-t-ch N-one-such!" cried Mr. Apple breathlessly. "She has been eating our a-pp-les."

Mac and Jon began to run, too. Mac ran one way among the apple trees, and Jon ran the other way. Nonesuch ran faster than ever around and around the apple trees, but she could not run away from Mac. She could not run away from Jon. The boys were too quick for her. Finally, Mac caught hold of her head, and Jon caught hold of her short tail. Then Mr. Apple was so exhausted from running that he sat right down on the ground under the nearest apple tree.

"This will never do, Jonathan," said Mr. Apple, who always used the children's full apple names when anything really serious happened. "This will never do, MacIntosh," went on Mr. Apple. "Nonesuch must not eat our apples. We have to sell the apples to help pay for the house. You will have to give her back to Farmer Gray."

"Oh, Father," said Jon sadly.

"Oh, Father," said Mac.

"Nonesuch must not eat our apples," said Mr. Apple again very firmly. "We need every one."

"I know what I can do," said Jon. "I will tie her up when I am not here to watch her. May I keep her then, Father?"

"Very well," said Mr. Apple, who was really very fond of Nonesuch. "If you keep her tied up until all the apples are picked, you may keep her."

"Are the apples ripe enough to pick now?" asked Jon.

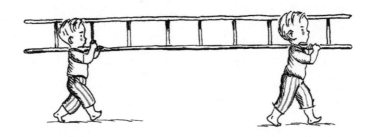

"Yes," said Mr. Apple. "Tomorrow is Saturday, and I do not have to go to the city. We will pick the apples tomorrow."

"Hurrah!" said Mac.

"Hurrah!" said Jon. "We will not have to keep Nonesuch tied up for long."

The next morning, Mr. Apple and the boys got up very early. Right after breakfast, they went out to the apple orchard. Mac and Jon carried a ladder. Mr. Apple carried another ladder. Mrs. Apple, Delia, and Snow followed them, carrying empty baskets and pails to put the apples in. Baby Ann came along with them. She did not carry anything. She was too little.

106

Mac and Jon put their ladder up against a tree. Mr. Apple put his ladder up against another tree. Mac ran up his ladder to the very top of the apple tree. He began to pick apples. He picked them very fast and dropped them down to Delia, who held out her pail to catch the apples as they fell.

"No, no," called Mr. Apple to Mac. "That is not the way to pick apples. You should pick the apples on the low branches first. You will bruise the apples lower down on the tree. Then we cannot sell them. Hang a pail on your ladder and put each apple in the pail carefully."

"I see," said Mac. "I will come down further and pick the low apples first. I will put them in the pail carefully."

All day Mr. Apple and Mac and Jon picked

apples. They picked them very carefully. Mrs. Apple, Delia, and Snow packed them in baskets. Baby Ann watched them. "Apples, apples," she said over and over.

"Hats full and caps full
Baskets and bags full
See our apples round and red,"

sang Delia and Snow as they worked.

Nonesuch was tied to the fence. "Maa, maa," she said as she watched the apple pickers.

Clover was nibbling his favorite red clover blossoms nearby. Every little while he stopped nibbling to look at the apple pickers.

"Baa, baa," he said.

At noon Mrs. Apple brought sandwiches and a big pitcher of milk into the apple orchard.

"Hurrah!" said Mac.

"Hurrah!" said Jon.

"Hurrah! Hurrah!" said Delia and Snow.

All the Apples sat down under the apple trees to eat lunch. They were very hungry. They ate and ate and ate. Jon gave Nonesuch one of his peanut butter sandwiches, and Mac gave Clover one of his jelly sandwiches.

"Maa, maa," said Nonesuch.

"Baa, baa," said Clover.

After lunch Mr. Apple and the boys went back to work again. By the time the sun was ready to set, all the apples were picked from the little apple trees. Mr. Apple covered the baskets up tight so that Nonesuch could not eat any more apples.

"On Monday you boys can take the apples to Mr. Jake. He will carry them to town in his wagon for us and sell them at the market," said Mr. Apple.

"Nonesuch can help us," said Jon happily. "We can put a basket of apples in our little wagon, and she can draw it down to Mr. Jake's store."

"That is a fine idea," said Mr. Apple.

On Monday morning Mac and Jon began to load their wagon with apples. Back and forth all day went Nonesuch, drawing baskets of apples in the wagon. Back and forth to Mr. Jake's store went Mac and Jon, driving the wagon.

At last all the apples were delivered to Mr. Jake. He loaded his big wagon with all the baskets of red apples.

"Hop on," said Mr. Jake to the boys. "You may ride to town with me."

"Hurrah!" said Mac.

"Hurrah!" said Jon. "I will take Nonesuch home first and come right back."

Soon Jon was back, and both boys climbed up on the wagon.

"Giddy up," said Mr. Jake to his horses, and

113

off they all started for town with a big, big load of red apples to sell.

That night when Mr. Apple came home, Mac and Jon ran down the lane to meet him. Delia and Snow ran to meet him, too. Mrs. Apple stood by the gate watching them with Baby Ann beside her. Nonesuch and Clover scampered after the Apple children.

"Father," called Mac. "Here is the money. Here is the money for the apples."

"Good boys," said Mr. Apple. "Now I am sure we will be able to buy the house. Soon the house will be our own home, and the apple orchard will be all our own, too. We will spray the trees carefully so that each year we will have good apples to sell. Then it will not be long before we have paid all the money for the house."

"Nonesuch helped us," said Mac.

"Nonesuch carried all the apples to Mr. Jake's store," said Jon.

"Good for Nonesuch," said Mr. Apple. He reached in his pocket and brought out a bag of candy. He gave a piece of candy to Nonesuch.

"Maa, maa," said Nonesuch.

"Clover would have helped, too, if he could," said Mac.

Mr. Apple gave some candy to Clover, too.

"Baa, baa," said Clover.

That night Mr. and Mrs. Apple were very happy. Mac and Jon and Delia and Snow were happy, too. Ann Apple was very happy, too, though she did not understand why. She was too little to understand about selling apples and buying houses.

After supper the Apple family went out to the apple orchard. They took hold of hands and danced around the apple trees, singing their favorite song:

> *"Sing hail to thee*
> *Old apple tree."*

117

They danced and danced and sang and sang until they could not dance anymore. Then they went into the house and went to bed.

Soon the cold winds of autumn came. They blew around the little red house. They blew the leaves off the trees in the apple orchard. Snowflakes covered the green roof of the little red house in the apple orchard.

Mr. and Mrs. Apple and their five little Apples were cozy and warm in the little red house until spring came and the apple trees were covered with little pink blossoms once more.

The End